The Happy Prince

and other stories

Edited by Vic Parker

Miles Kelly PUBLISHING

Contents

Ricky with the Tuft   7
Illustrated by Cecilia Johansson

The Happy Prince   13
Illustrated by Pam Smy

Baba Yaga   19
Illustrated by Julie Banyard

The Selfish Giant   24
Illustrated by Peter Utton

A Tall Story
Illustrated by Peter Utton
28

The Moon in the Pond
Illustrated by Caroline Sharpe
30

Rip Van Winkle
Illustrated by Susan Scott
35

The Nutcracker Prince
Illustrated by Julie Banyard
40

The Fisherman and the Bottle
Illustrated by Susan Scott
45

The Happy Prince

and other stories

First published in 2001 by Miles Kelly Publishing,
Bardfield Centre, Great Bardfield, Essex CM7 4SL

Printed in China

Project manager: Paula Borton
Editorial Assistant: Isla MacCuish

British Library Cataloguing-in-Publication Data
A catalogue record for this book is available from the British Library

ISBN 1-84236-060-4

24681097531

Visit us on the web:
www.mileskelly.net
Info@mileskelly.net

RICKY WITH THE TUFT

retold from the original story by Charles Perrault

Aaaarrggh!" cried the queen, as she saw her newborn son for the first time. "Surely this baby can't be mine! He's hideously ugly!"

The fairy midwife sighed. It was true. The tiny face of the queen's new baby boy was swamped by a huge red nose. He was cross-eyed and his shoulders were humped. One of his legs was much shorter than the other. And to top it all, the baby was totally bald except for a single tuft of hair sticking up in the middle of his head. "Never mind your little boy's looks, your majesty," the fairy midwife comforted the queen. "I promise that your son will grow up to be far more intelligent, witty and charming than other people, and everyone will love him for it. What's more, I'm going to give him a gift. I'm going to give him the power to make the girl he falls in love with as intelligent as he is, so he won't ever get bored with her company . . . Now, what are you going to call your special little son?"

"Ricky . . ." the queen decided, making up her mind that she loved her son after all. "He's my little Ricky with the Tuft."

Not long afterwards, the queen of a neighbouring kingdom

gave birth to twin daughters. The first tiny girl to be born was so perfect that the queen at first thought she was looking at a little angel from heaven. But the second baby was as ugly as her elder sister was beautiful.

"Oh dear," said the fairy midwife – the same one who had helped at the birth of Ricky with the Tuft. "I have to tell you that your elder daughter will grow up to be incrediby stupid . . . However, there is some comfort. Your younger daughter will stay ugly, but she will be so clever that no one will even notice."

The queen was relieved that her younger daughter's fate seemed to be taken care of, but she was very worried about her elder daughter. "Can't we somehow give the elder one some of the younger one's intelligence?" the queen suggested.

"I'm afraid that's beyond my powers," the fairy midwife replied. "However, what I can do for her is to make her more beautiful than any girl in the world. What's more, I'll also give her a gift. The boy she falls in love with will become as beautiful as she is, so she'll never tire of looking at him."

Sixteen or so years passed, and the two princesses grew up exactly as the fairy midwife had said they would. Strangers were at first entranced by the beauty of the elder princess. However, they would soon creep away because trying to make conversation with her was as difficult as digging a field with a spoon. The strangers would then turn to the younger princess and be captivated by her intelligent and entertaining chat. Everyone totally forgot how plain and ungainly the princess was after only five minutes in her enchanting company.

Unfortunately, the beautiful elder sister knew very well that she was exceedingly stupid and embarrassing. She often stole away into the woods to be on her own – and it was on one of these lonely walks that she first encountered Ricky with the Tuft.

It wasn't an accident that the princess and the prince came to meet each other. Ricky with the Tuft had fallen desperately in love with the pictures of the princess that were for sale in all the shops. After collecting every single one, sticking them all over his bedroom walls, and gazing at them adoringly for hours on end, Ricky with the Tuft had decided that he wanted to marry the real thing. He had set off determined to find her.

"My lady, I feel as if I have been looking for you all my life," sighed Ricky with the Tuft, bowing low to the princess.

The princess just shrugged, as she couldn't think of anything to

say to the remarkably ugly prince who stood before her.

"I have never seen a girl as beautiful as you," admitted Ricky with the Tuft. "And as I should know more than most, beauty is an important blessing that shouldn't be taken for granted."

The sad princess blurted out, "I would much rather be as ugly as you are, if only I could be a little less stupid!"

Luckily, Ricky with the Tuft wasn't offended. "I have the perfect solution," he smiled. "I love you with all my heart, and if you will only consent to be my wife, you will become as wise and witty as you could ever wish to be."

The princess wasn't sure if she understood or not what the ugly prince was saying. She stood gaping open-mouthed.

"I can see you are a little taken aback by the suddenness of my proposal," said Ricky with the Tuft, kindly. "So I will give you a whole year to get used to the idea."

The princess said nothing to disagree, and so Ricky with the Tuft trotted off home, his heart full to bursting with happiness.

From that moment on, the princess discovered that she was as intelligent and entertaining as she was beautiful. The news spread rapidly, and princes and lords and earls came from kingdoms far and wide to seek her hand in marriage. Of course, in all the excitement, the princess quite forgot about Ricky with the Tuft. Her mind was completely taken up with one big worry. The princess thought each suitor very handsome in his own way, but now that she herself was so clever, she found them all extremely boring! "How can I marry a man whose conversation sends me to sleep within five minutes?" she sighed wistfully.

One day, the princess decided to wander alone into the woods to think the problem over. She hadn't been gone long when she came

across a hundred servants preparing a banquet among the trees. They were hanging flags and balloons and coloured lanterns in the branches; they were scurrying to and fro in a vast outdoor kitchen, cooking a delicious feast; they were setting up a dance floor and a bandstand, and laying thousands of tables and chairs – all beautifully decked with flowers. "Whatever is going on?" the astounded princess asked one of the servants. She had attended many wonderful balls, but had never been to one on such a grand, gorgeous scale. "The person giving this banquet must have a very important reason to throw such a wonderful party."

"Tomorrow our master, Ricky with the Tuft, is getting married," the breathless servant replied. "He loves his bride with all his heart and is throwing the best wedding feast ever!"

The princess gasped as she suddenly remembered the squinting, limping, hunchbacked prince with the huge nose and the strange tuft of hair, whom she had met exactly a year before. *I gave him the impression I would marry him!* she thought in horror.

The princess suddenly saw Ricky with the Tuft himself heading through the trees towards her. "Good afternoon, my darling," he cried. "I have kept my word and have come to see how you feel about marrying me now."

The princess hung her head in shame. "There is no doubt in my mind that you are the kindest, most honourable, most intelligent person in the world," she sobbed. "I would love to be with you forever – but I can't! I am deeply sorry that I can never marry you, for I can't get over your terrible ugliness!"

To the princess's amazement, Ricky with the Tuft laughed out loud. "Well, I do believe that you've fallen in love with me after all," he cried. And when the princess looked up, she saw that Ricky with the Tuft had become as handsome as she herself was beautiful. "Didn't you know you had the power to do that?" the prince beamed.

The princess fell into his arms, and the very next day, she and her prince had the best wedding feast ever - just as Ricky with the Tuft had wanted.

THE HAPPY PRINCE

retold from the original tale by Oscar Wilde

The statue of the Happy Prince stood high up above the city on a tall column. He glittered in the sunlight, for he was painted all over in gold leaf and had a glowing ruby set into his sword hilt and two sparkling sapphires for eyes. The people of the city often looked up at the Happy Prince and sighed, for they admired his beauty and envied his contented smile.

One evening, a little swallow came fluttering through the skies and landed between the prince's golden feet. It was well past the end of the summer and the wind had grown chill. The swallow's friends had set off several weeks ago for a warmer land. The swallow had stayed behind because he had fallen in love with a slender reed by the river, and he could not bear to leave her. But the wind had grown chill and the bite of frost had crept into the air. The shivering swallow had realised that to stay any longer would mean certain death from the cold. He had begged the reed to travel with him, but the reed had

simply shaken her
head. So the swallow
had been forced to fly sadly
off without her. Tomorrow he
would fly away and catch up with his
friends. Now the little bird tucked his head
under his wing and prepared to get some rest for the
long journey. But just as the swallow began to drift off into dreams,
large raindrops started to fall on his head. The swallow looked up in
puzzlement at the clear night sky and saw that the statue above him
was crying.

"Who are you and why are you weeping?" the little swallow
asked, as the statue's tears shone in the moonlight like diamonds.

"People call me the Happy Prince," replied the statue, "but in
truth, I am full of sadness. They have set me up here so high that I
can look out over the whole city and see all its ugliness and misery.
Tonight, I can see a poor woman sitting in a house near the edge of
town. The woman is thin from hunger and pale from tiredness, but
she is still at work, sewing passion-flowers onto a gown for one of
the queen's maids-of-honour. In the corner of the room, her little boy
lies very ill in bed, asking for oranges. But the woman has no money

to buy him anything, so all she can give him is water." The Happy Prince sighed. "Little swallow, will you pluck out the ruby from my sword and take it to the woman, so that she might sell it to the jeweller for money? My feet are fastened to this pedestal and I cannot move."

The Happy Prince looked so sad that the swallow agreed to be his messenger. The little bird pecked the ruby out of the prince's sword and flew away with it in his beak over the rooftops. He flew in at the window of the woman's house and found her slumped over her work in a worn-out sleep. The swallow laid the jewel down next to her thimble, then he flew gently round the bed, fanning the feverish, sick boy with his wings until he looked much cooler and more comfortable. Then the swallow flew back to the Happy Prince and told him what he had done. "It's strange," the bird remarked. "I feel a warm glow inside me, even though the weather is so cold."

"That is because you have done a good deed," explained the Happy Prince, as the tired little swallow closed his eyes.

Next day, the swallow flew all over the city bidding goodbye to everyone and everything. "I am leaving tonight for Egypt!" he cried. But when in the evening he came to say farewell to the Happy Prince, he found that the statue was crying once again.

"Far across the city I can see into an attic where a young man leans over a desk. He is struggling to finish a play for the Director of the Theatre, but he is too cold to write anymore. His fire has died away and he has no money to buy either wood or any food for his supper." A glistening tear rolled off the end of the Happy Prince's nose and sploshed onto the swallow's head. "Little swallow, will you stay with me one more night and be my messenger? Will you pluck out one of my sapphire eyes and take it to him?"

"Dear prince," said the swallow, "I will not pluck out your eye." and tears gleamed in his own.

"Little swallow, please do as I ask," begged the Happy Prince, and he looked so sad that the swallow fluttered up and plucked out one of his sapphire eyes and flew away with it to the young man in the attic. The little swallow was very relieved when he returned to nestle at the Happy Prince's feet, for the air underneath his wings had really become very cold indeed.

The next day, the swallow flew down to the harbour and watched all the big ships sailing away to lands where the breezes were warm and the days were long. "I am leaving too, tonight!" he sang out to everyone he saw. At sunset, the swallow flew off to the Happy Prince to say goodbye. "In the square below," said the Happy Prince, "I can see a little matchgirl whose matches have all spilled into the gutter. She is crying because she can make no money and if she goes home empty-handed, her father will beat her." The Happy Prince smiled sadly. "Little swallow, pluck out my other eye and take it to the little matchgirl so she can be happy."

"But then you will be blind!" cried the swallow.

"Little swallow, please do as I ask," whispered the Happy Prince, and he looked so sad that the bird did as he wanted.

"Now you can no longer see," the little swallow said, as he fluttered back to the statue. "I will stay with you always."

"But little swallow," protested the Happy Prince, "your friends will be waiting for you on the hazy banks of the River Nile."

"I will stay with you always and be your eyes," the swallow promised, and he slept between the prince's feet.

Next day, the swallow flew all over the city and told the Happy Prince what he had seen there. "I have seen the rich making merry in their beautiful houses while beggars lie outside their gates," the swallow murmured. "I have seen old people who sit all day on their own, cold and lonely. I have seen small children tremble in front of bullies. I have seen much suffering and misery."

"Little swallow," said the prince, "with your beak, peel off the fine gold that covers me. Fly with leaves of it to all the poor people of my city."

The little swallow sighed heavily, but he did what he was told. Then the statue of the Happy Prince was quite dull and grey.

As the faithful bird finally settled down between his friend's feet, the snow began to fall in thick white flakes. The streets glistened silver with a lining of frost. Icicles hung like shards of glass from the rooftops. And the little swallow shivered at the foot of the Happy Prince. He tried beating his wings to keep warm, but eventually he knew that he was going to die. The little swallow used his last drop of strength to flutter up to the prince's shoulder. "Goodbye, Happy Prince," he cried. "I will not see you again."

"I am glad you are finally going to where the sun will warm your wings," the Happy Prince said.

"I am not going to Egypt," murmured the swallow, "I am going to sleep forever." And he kissed the Happy Prince on the lips and fell down dead at his feet.

That very moment, a strange cracking noise came from within the Happy Prince. It was so loud that the Mayor heard it way down below. He peered up at the statue for the first time in months. "Good lord!" he remarked. "However did the Happy Prince get that shabby? We'll have to replace him with something else."

The very next day, workmen pulled down the Happy Prince from his column and threw him into a furnace. They cleared away the dead swallow and then put a statue of the Mayor on the column instead. But the Happy Prince knew nothing about all this, because his heart had broken. In fact, when the workmen opened the door of the furnace, they saw his cracked lead heart for themselves, because it would not melt away. They threw it onto the same rubbish dump on which they had thrown the dead swallow was lying. And when God asked his angels to bring him the two most precious things in all the city, they took the Happy Prince's heart and the little swallow with them up to heaven.

BABA YAGA, THE BONY-LEGGED

a Russian folk tale

There was once a wicked woman who hated her stepdaughter so much that she pushed the little girl out of doors and told her to go and borrow a needle and thread from Baba Yaga, the bony-legged witch. The girl's stepmother did it when her husband was out at work, so the little girl had no one to turn to and she was terrified. Baba Yaga had iron teeth, and lived in the middle of the deep, dark forest, in a hut which moved about on hens' legs. Neverthless, the girl dared not disobey her cruel stepmother. So off she went into the deep, dark forest.

The little girl was soon among tall, prickly trees that whispered all around her, and she quite forgot which way was which. Big tears began to glisten in her eyes.

"Do not weep, little girl," came a cheerful voice. The little girl looked up to see that a little nightingale was talking to her. "You are a kind-hearted girl and I will tell you what I can to help you. Pick up any things that you come across along the path and make sure you use them wisely."

So the little girl set off again, further into the deep, dark forest.

As she walked along, she saw a neatly folded handkerchief lying among the pine-needles, and she put it in her pocket. A little further on, she took some ribbons that were dangling from the branches. A few steps on, she picked up a little can of oil that lay amongst some rocks. Next, she came across a big, juicy bone and then a large maple-leaf sprinkled with some tasty-looking morsels of meat – and then her pocket was full.

It wasn't long before some big iron gates came into view up ahead, and beyond them was Baba Yaga's hut, running about on its hens' legs. The little girl shivered with fear. Suddenly a howling wind rose up which sent the branches of the trees whipping fiercely around her head. *I'll never get near that horrible hut at this rate*, the little girl realised, ducking the boughs coming at her thick and fast. She thought quickly. She pulled out the ribbons and tied them onto the trees, and as soon as she did so, the wind dropped to a gentle breeze and the branches became still.

Then the little girl tried to push open the gates, but a dreadful creaking and groaning tore the air. The girl took the oil can from her pocket and gave the hinges a good oiling. After that, the gate opened without a squeak, and the girl passed through.

All of a sudden, a drooling, snarling dog came running at her out of nowhere, barking fit to wake the dead. Quick as a flash, the girl grabbed the big, juicy bone and threw it to the dog. He forgot his attack immediately and lay down and began to gnaw.

Now the girl faced the hut itself, scuttling about on its awful scaly legs. And there on the steps stood BABA YAGA THE BONY-LEGGED! "Come in, my dear!" grinned the witch, showing her iron teeth. "While I'm searching for that needle and thread you want, you can have a nice bath and do my spinning for me."

Baba Yaga gripped the girl's arm with her claw-like fingers and pulled her up the steps into the house. "Run her a bath and be quick about it!" she screamed at her pale-faced maid, before whispering "Make sure you scrub her well, all ready for eating." Then Baba Yaga the bony-legged bustled away.

The pale-faced maid began to hurry about filling the bath with water, and the little girl saw that she was trembling with fear of Baba Yaga the bony-legged. "I am sorry for you having to live and work here," the little girl said. "Here, have this handkerchief as a little present to cheer you up."

"Oh thank you," the pale-faced maid sighed, gazing in delight at the lovely embroidery. "I will use a teacup instead of a jug to fill the bath, so you have more time to escape."

Then the little girl noticed a skinny black cat in the corner. "You don't look as if you've eaten properly for ages," she said, stroking his tatty fur. "Here, have these scraps of meat."

"Oh thank you," the skinny black cat purred, neatly washing his paws. "I will do the spinning for you, so you have more time to escape. Now take this magic towel and comb and run for your life. When you hear Baba Yaga coming, throw each of them behind you, one by one."

So the little girl took the magic towel and comb and began to run for her life through the deep, dark forest, while the cat sat down at the spinning wheel, tangled the wool into a big mess and hid behind it, and began to spin.

Several times, the witch passed the open door of the room and peered in. But when she heard the whirr of the spinning wheel and saw the pile of tangled wool, she went away content that the little girl was working hard. But by and by, the witch began to get suspicious that the pile of wool wasn't getting any smaller. "Are you sure you know how to spin properly, little girl?" she screeched.

"Yes, thank you," yowled the cat, trying to sound like the little girl but failing terribly. Then Baba Yaga the bony-legged screamed with fury. She rushed into the room and grabbed the cat by the scruff of the neck. "Why did you let the girl escape?" she howled.

"You've never given me anything to eat but left-overs," the cat hissed. "That kind-hearted girl gave me tasty morsels of meat."

Then Baba Yaga stalked over to the pale-faced maid and slapped her. "Why did you let the girl escape?" she howled.

"You've never given me a single present," the pale-faced maid shouted. "That kind-hearted girl gave me a lovely hanky."

Then Baba Yaga stormed outside and threw a stick at the dog. "Why did you let the girl escape?" she howled.

"You've never given me a bone," the dog barked. "That kind-hearted girl gave me a big, juicy one to chew on."

Then Baba Yaga kicked the iron gates. "Why did you let the girl escape?" she howled.

"You've let us get all stiff and rusty," they creaked. "That kind-hearted girl soothed our aching joints with lots of lovely oil."

Finally, Baba Yaga punched the birch trees. "Why did you let the girl escape?" she howled.

"You've never once decorated our branches," they roared, "but that kind-hearted girl tied beautiful ribbons all over us."

Then Baba Yaga gnashed her iron teeth and jumped on her broomstick and raced off through the deep, dark forest after the little girl. The little girl heard the swish of the air and knew she was coming and threw down the magic towel. Suddenly a wide rushing river appeared before Baba Yaga, splashing all over her broomstick and soaking it so badly that it could no longer fly. Spitting and cursing, Baba Yaga had to get off and slowly wade across. Then Baba Yaga was off and running . . .

The little girl heard the pounding of Baba Yaga's footsteps and knew she was coming, and she threw down the magic comb. All at once, a jungle sprang up in front of Baba Yaga, so thick and dense and tangled that Baba Yaga the bony-legged could do nothing to find her way through it. She squawked and screamed and gnashed her iron teeth, and stormed back to her horrible hut, shouting all the way.

The little girl saw her father standing at the door of their house, and she rushed to tell him all about her stepmother's evil plot. Her father pushed the wicked woman out of doors and drove her into the magic jungle – after which, she was never seen again. Then the little girl and her father lived happily on their own, and the nightingale came to visit every day.

THE SELFISH GIANT

retold from the original tale by Oscar Wilde

nce there was a beautiful garden in which the children used to play every day on their way home from school. The children didn't think that the beautiful garden belonged to anyone in particular. But one day a huge giant strode in and boomed, "What are you all doing here? This is MY garden. Get lost!" Seven years ago, the giant had gone to visit his friend the Cornish ogre. Now he was back and he wanted his garden all to himself.

Of course, the children ran away at once. But the giant wasn't satisfied. Straight away, he put up a high fence all the way around his garden with a noticeboard outside which read: TRESPASSERS WILL BE PROSECUTED. He really was a very selfish giant.

Now the poor children had nowhere to play. But the giant didn't give any thought to that. He was too busy wondering why the blossom had fallen from the trees, why the flowers had withered, and why all the birds seemed to have flown away. *Surely it is meant to be the springtime,* the giant thought to himself as he looked out of the window and saw huge flakes of snow beginning to tumble from the sky. Frost painted the trees silver. A blanket of ice chilled the ground and hardened the plants into stiff, lifeless spikes. Day after day, the north wind roared around the giant's garden, zooming around his roof and howling down his chimney pots. And the hail came to visit too, battering on the giant's windows until the giant bellowed with annoyance and clapped his hands over his ears against the noisy rattling.

Then one Saturday, the giant woke up to hear a sound he had almost forgotten – it was a bird, chirruping and cheeping in his garden. A beautiful perfume tickled the giant's nose . . . It was the scent of flowers! "Spring has come at last!" the giant beamed, and he pulled on his clothes and ran outside into his garden.

The giant couldn't believe what he saw. The snow had melted, the frost and ice were gone, the sky was blue and the breeze was gentle and warm. And there were children everywhere. They had crept back into his garden through a hole that had worn away in the fence. Now children were sitting in trees heavy with ripe fruit. Playing among flowerbeds filled with nodding blossoms.

Running over emerald green grass scattered with daisies and buttercups. And the sound of their happy laughter filled the air.

Only in one corner of the garden was it still winter. A little boy was standing in a patch of snow, looking up at the bare branches of a chestnut tree and crying because he couldn't reach it. The giant's heart ached as he watched. "Now I know what makes my garden beautiful," the giant murmured. "It is the children. How selfish I have been!"

The giant strode through the garden towards the sobbing little boy. The giant scooped him up gently and set him among the icy boughs of the chestnut tree. At once, broad green leaves appeared all over the branches and down below, the snow vanished and it was spring. The little boy's face brightened into a huge smile and he reached his arms up around the giant's neck and hugged him.

"It is your garden now, little children," laughed the giant, and the children skipped about delightedly. The giant took his axe and knocked down the fence and had more fun than he had ever had in his life by playing with them all day. Only one thing spoiled the giant's new happiness. He looked all over his garden for the little boy whom he had helped into the tree, but he was nowhere to be found. The giant loved the little boy the best, because he had kissed him, and he longed more than anything to see his friend again.

Many years passed by and the children came every day to play in the beautiful garden. The giant became old and creaky and eventually he could no longer run about and let the children climb over him as he had done. The giant sat in a special armchair so he could watch the children enjoying themselves. "My garden is very beautiful," he would say to himself, 'but the children are the most beautiful things of all." Sometimes the giant's huge grey head would nod forwards and he would begin to snore, and the children would creep away quietly so they didn't disturb him. And one afternoon, the giant woke from such a little doze to see an astonishing sight.

In the farthest corner of his garden was a golden tree he had never seen before. The giant's heart leaped for joy, for standing underneath it was the little boy he had loved.

The giant heaved himself up from his armchair and shuffled across the grass as fast as his old legs would take him. But when he drew near the little boy, his face grew black as thunder. There were wounds on the little boy's palms and on his feet. "Who has dared to hurt you?" boomed the giant. "Tell me, and I will go after them with my big axe!"

"These are the marks of love," the little boy smiled, and he took the giant's hand. "Once, you let me play in your garden," the little boy said. "And today, you shall come with me to mine, which is in Paradise."

And when the children came running to play that afternoon, they found the giant lying dead under the beautiful tree, covered with a blanket of snowy-white blossoms.

A TALL STORY

an Indian folk tale

Five blind men were once sitting under a shady palm tree by the bank of the River Ganges in India, when they sensed that someone or something had silently crept up and joined them. "Who's there?" asked the first blind man. There was no reply, so he got to his feet and walked forwards with his arms outstretched. After a few steps, his hands hit something flat and rough and solid in front of him. "It's a wall!" he cried, triumphantly.

"Don't be stupid!" cried the second blind man, standing up. "How could someone have built a wall right under our noses without us hearing?" He, too, felt about in front of him. "Aha!" he said, delightedly, as he ran his hands down a hard, smooth, stick-like thing. "It's a spear, definitely a spear!"

At that, the third blind man got up to join them. "A wall and a spear!" he sneered. "Obviously, neither of you have any idea what this thing is." His fingers closed around something tatty and wiggly. "It's nothing more than a piece of old rope!" he laughed.

"How can you say that?" argued the fourth blind man, who had jumped up and joined in without anyone noticing. "I'm standing here with my arms wrapped around something so big that my fingers are barely touching together. It's a tree trunk, I'm telling you. A tree trunk!"

"I suppose I'll have to settle this," sniffed the fifth blind man, as he rose. He stuck out his hand confidently and grabbed hold of something long and swaying. "HELP!" he shouted. "It's a snake! It's a snake!"

Suddenly, whoops of laughter filled the air and the five blind men heard a little boy giggle, "You're ALL wrong! You're actually holding parts of an elephant – and you all look REALLY SILLY!"

At that, the first blind man stopped patting the elephant's side. The second blind man stopped stroking the elephant's tusk. The third blind man stopped holding the elephant's tail. The fourth blind man stopped hugging the elephant's leg. And the fifth blind man let go of the elephant's trunk. And from that moment on, the five blind men never argued again.

THE MOON IN THE POND

retold from the original tale by Uncle Remus

E very now and again Brer Fox and Brer Rabbit would shake
hands and make peace for a while and, following their
example, all the critters would forget their arguments and
get along together just dandy. It had been like this for some weeks
when Brer Rabbit ran into Brer Turtle and they got talking.

"It sure is peaceful around here now," sighed Brer Rabbit.

"Yep," nodded Brer Turtle, who was a man of few words.

"It sure is quiet," sighed Brer Rabbit.

"Yep," nodded Brer Turtle.

"Peaceful and quiet is good, but it ain't fun like in the old days,
is it Brer Turtle?" asked Brer Rabbit.

"Nope," agreed Brer Turtle.

"I think that the folks round here could do with a dose of fun
again," sighed Brer Rabbit.

"Yep," nodded Brer Turtle.

Brer Rabbit bounced to his feet with a chuckle. "Then I'm going
to invite everyone to a little fishing frolic at the pond tomorrow
night," he said. "I'll do all the talking as long as you back me up with

your 'yep' and 'nope' now and then." And Brer Rabbit and Brer Turtle shook hands. Brer Rabbit loped off to do the inviting and Brer Turtle set out for the pond, so as he'd be sure to get there on time . . .

Sure enough, the following night, everyone was there at the pond. Brer Bear and Brer Wolf had brought their hooks and lines. Brer Turtle carried a pot of wriggling bait. Brer Fox brought his fishing net.

Miss Meadows and Miss Motts brought themselves, dressed up to the nines.

While Brer Turtle shook his pot at Miss Meadows and Miss Motts and made them squeal with delight, Brer Bear announced he was going to fish for mud-cats. Brer Wolf said he was going to fish for horneyheads. Brer Fox declared he was going to fish for perch for the ladies. And Brer Rabbit winked at Brer Turtle and said he was going to fish for suckers.

So everyone got busy with their hooks and their lines and their bait, and Brer Rabbit went to cast his line first. "I don't believe it!" he gasped, peering into the water and scratching his head. "The moon has done gone and fell in the water!"

Everyone looked serious and gathered round and tut-tutted and well-welled and my-myed as they looked into the pond and saw the moon floating there like a big pale coin. "There ain't no fish gonna come swimmin' through this water unless we get the moon out of the way," said Brer Rabbit. "Isn't that so, Brer Turtle?"

"Yep," nodded Brer Turtle, with a twinkle in his eye.

"So how we gonna get the moon out, Brer Rabbit?" worried Miss Meadows.

"Hmm," pondered Brer Rabbit, thoughtfully. "I've got it! We borrow Brer Turtle's drag net, and we drag it across the pond, and we drag the moon right out!"

"That's it!" breathed everyone, excitedly.

"That's surely it!"

"It don't bother you none if we borrow your drag net, does it Brer Turtle?" asked Brer Rabbit.

"Nope," replied Brer Turtle, trying hard not to collapse into laughter.

Then Brer Rabbit leapt off to fetch Brer Turtle's drag net and was back again before anyone could say 'lickety-spit'. "I think I'd better be the one to do the dragging," Brer Rabbit sighed. "It needs someone mighty clever and mighty muscley."

At that, Brer Fox and Brer Bear and Brer Wolf sprang forward and insisted on taking the drag net from Brer Rabbit. After all, they didn't want to look like saps in front of the ladies, now, did they?

Brer Fox and Brer Bear and Brer Wolf walked gingerly down to the edge of the pond with the net. They cast it into the water, dragged it along, and heaved it out, dripping. When the ripples had settled on the pond, there was the moon, shining just as bright in the water as before.

"Nope!" cried Brer Rabbit. "You need to go deeper."

Brer Fox and Brer Bear and Brer Wolf waded knee-deep into the cold pond. Once again they cast out the drag net, and once again they pulled it in without having caught the moon.

"Try again a little deeper," yelled Brer Rabbit from the nice, dry bank. "You'll surely get it next time." And Miss Meadows and Miss Motts eagerly waved them further out.

Brer Fox and Brer Bear and Brer Wolf took one more step and

suddenly the bottom of the pond fell away steeply and there was no more mud under their feet and they were ducked right under the water! Up they popped, choking and splashing and spluttering.

Miss Meadows and Miss Motts giggled and snickered as Brer Fox and Brer Bear and Brer Wolf hauled themselves out of the pond. They were a sight for sore eyes, dripping water from every hair and covered all-over in waterweed.

I've heard that the moon will always bite if you use fools for bait, Brer Rabbit giggled, looking them up and down. Now if you're asking me, "you gentlemen ought to get yourselves home and into some dry clothes,". And as Brer Fox and Brer Bear and Brer Wolf slopped and slapped away into the moonlight, Brer Turtle and Brer Rabbit went home with the girls.

RIP VAN WINKLE

an American legend

In a village in the foothills of the Catskill Mountains of America lived a man called Rip Van Winkle.

Everybody liked Rip. He was a generous, easy-going man who was always glad to lend a hand to his neighbours. In fact, Rip Van Winkle was always to be found doing anybody else's work except his own. And didn't his wife remind him about it all the time! Nag, nag, nag it was, all day long. "Rip, if you're not too busy varnishing Mrs Green's fence today, you can mend the holes in the shed. Instead of helping to burn the farmer's rubbish, you can feed the chickens and milk the cows. Then if you can stop yourself from building Arne Jacob's wall for him, there's our potatoes to dig up and the wagon to be washed down and the gutters to be cleared out and the yard to be swept and . . ." And so it was every day, on and on and on and on.

Every now and again, Rip Van Winkle whistled for his faithful dog Wolf, shouldered his gun, and strode away from his wife without a word. Off he would stroll up the mountainside, along the river and through the pine forests until his wife's screeching voice had

grown so faint that he could no longer hear it, and he was surrounded only by the twittering of the birds, the rustling of the trees in the breeze and the panting of his companion by his side. Rip always knew there would be heck to pay when he got home. But a day off in the peaceful sunshine was well worth it!

One day when Rip had disappeared on one of these rambles, he was taking a rest under a shady tree, when he heard a voice calling his name. "Rip Van Winkle! Rip Van Winkle! Rip Van Winkle!" came the high, shrill cry.

Wolf's ears flattened against his skull and he gave a long, low growl. Rip looked in the direction Wolf was snarling and there among the long grass was a nodding green feather. The nodding green feather was tucked into a bright red cap. The cap was on the head of a bearded man no higher than his own boot, struggling under the weight of a big beer barrel.

"Rip Van Winkle! Rip Van Winkle! Rip Van Winkle!" shouted the dwarf, crossly. "Will you get yourself over here and give me a hand with this barrel before it squashes me!"

Rip was so used to doing what he was told that he jumped up to help at once.

"That's better," wheezed the dwarf, as Rip took one end of the heavy barrel. "Now up we go!" Rip nearly tripped over as the dwarf stomped away up the mountain, pulling the barrel and Rip Van Winkle with him.

After at least an hour's tramping and much huffing and puffing, the dwarf led Rip Van Winkle straight behind a thundering waterfall, through a hidden door and into an enormous cavern.

Dwarfs were swarming everywhere. Some were dressed in aprons, pouring endless tankards of beer out of big kegs just like the one Rip was helping to carry. Others were playing nine pins, rolling smooth round black rocks at copper skittles and cheering loudly. Yet more dwarfs were drinking and clinking their tankards together, singing noisy songs.

"Pull up a chair," Rip's new friend invited him, lowering the barrel to the floor and passing him a tankard. "Help yourself to a drink. You must be gasping thirsty after that climb – I know I am!"

The stunned Rip Van Winkle did just that. "My, that's mighty powerful stuff!" he spluttered, as he swallowed down a huge gulp of the dwarf beer. "But whatever it is, it's very good!" He licked his lips and poured himself another tankardful. None of the dwarfs was taking a blind bit of notice of him, so Rip Van Winkle sat back and began to watch the nine pins competition. "Well, this is a most pleasant way to spend the afternoon," he thought, helping himself to another beer . . . and another . . . and another . . . and another. And before Rip Van Winkle even realised he was drunk, he had slumped forwards onto a huge flat rock and was snoring loudly.

When Rip woke up, the dwarfs were gone and the cavern was empty. "Come on, Wolf," he yawned, and they both stood up and stretched. "We'd better hurry back or we'll never hear the last of it." Through the little door they strode and out from behind the waterfall and off down the mountain. "Wait for it," he murmured to his dog as he climbed the porch steps to his house. "Any minute now, that wife of mine will start screeching fit to wake the dead." Rip put his hand on the doorknob and turned. He nearly walked smack-bang into the door as it failed to open. "Well, this needs a bit of oil," he murmured to himself. He rattled the knob and twisted it about. "Funny," Rip remarked, "I think it's locked. She never locks the door, never."

At that very moment, the front door opened and there stood a woman with an angry face. "Who are you?" the woman snapped.

"What are you up to, trying to get in my front door?" She was not his wife. In fact, Rip Van Winkle had never seen her before.

"Who are you?" gasped Rip. "What are you doing in my house?"

"*Your* house!" the woman scoffed. "I've lived here for over nineteen years!"

Rip Van Winkle backed off the porch and looked around him. He scratched his head and stared. The woman was right – it *wasn't* his house. Well, it looked similar to his house, but the curtains at the window were different. There were strange chairs on the verandah. The wagon in the yard was not his wagon.

"But – I – How –" stuttered Rip. "Where's Mrs Van Winkle?"

"Mrs Van Winkle?" the puzzled woman gawped. "She left here nearly twenty years ago, just after her husband wandered off and disappeared. Now, be off with you or I'll call the police!"

"*Twenty years!*" marvelled Rip Van Winkle, as he wandered away stroking his beard. His beard! Suddenly Rip realised that his beard hung down to his knees. The woman's words had to be true! He had been asleep for twenty years!

Rip Van Winkle's hands trembled with the shock as he reached down and patted the bemused Wolf comfortingly. Then his mouth began to curve upwards in a small smile. "Just imagine, Wolf," he murmured. "No more nagging – ever!" Rip Van Winkle turned and strode across the street, whistling a merry tune. Happily, the inn was in the same place it always had been – and when the townspeople heard his story, he never had to buy himself another pint of beer again.

THE NUTCRACKER PRINCE

retold from the original tale by Ernst Hoffmann

r Drosselmeier was an old man with a secret. In his youth, he had been the most nimble-fingered, highly skilled craftsman in the entire royal court. Dr Drosselmeier had made clocks that were mechanical wonders. Some chimed with a hundred tinkling bells. Others were decorated with tiny musicians that danced and played their instruments as they struck the hour. Some even had secret doors, out of which little birds fluttered and flew around the room, chirruping the passing minutes. Yes, Dr Drosselmeier's clocks had been the talk of the palace. But the most amazing thing he had ever made was a mouse-trap.

Dr Drosselmeier had invented a brilliant clockwork trap that caught mice in their hundreds, twenty-four hours a day. Everyone in the palace had been delighted – except for the Mouse King. He too had lived in the palace with his subjects. Now, he was forced to leave and find another home, and he was furious about it. The Mouse King knew powerful magic and he took his revenge on Dr Drosselmeier by turning his nephew into an ugly, wooden doll.

The doll wore a painted soldier's uniform and it had a prince's crown

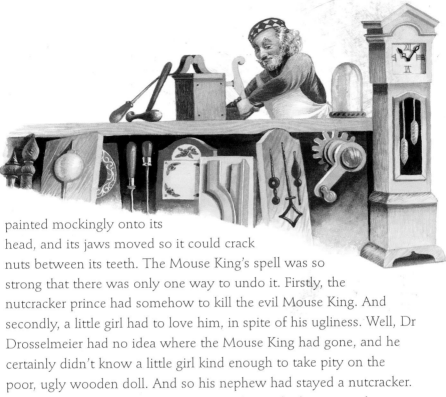

painted mockingly onto its
head, and its jaws moved so it could crack
nuts between its teeth. The Mouse King's spell was so
strong that there was only one way to undo it. Firstly, the
nutcracker prince had somehow to kill the evil Mouse King. And
secondly, a little girl had to love him, in spite of his ugliness. Well, Dr
Drosselmeier had no idea where the Mouse King had gone, and he
certainly didn't know a little girl kind enough to take pity on the
poor, ugly wooden doll. And so his nephew had stayed a nutcracker.

From that moment on, Dr Drosselmeier had never made
another clock. He lost all heart for mechanical things and so he lost
his job at the palace, too. Dr Drosselmeier blamed himself entirely for
his nephew's dreadful disappearance and he had never breathed a
word of what had happened to anyone. But ever since, he had been
trying to find a way to break the Mouse King's spell . . . and at last,
he thought he had.

Dr Drosselmeier's goddaughter, Clara, had grown into the
kindest little girl anyone could wish to meet. If any little girl was
going to take pity on the stiff, glaring nutcracker prince, it would
be Clara.

Now it was Christmas Eve, and Dr Drosselmeier had arrived at Clara's house trembling with excitement. He wasn't excited because there was a party going on with games and music and dancing. No, Dr Drosselmeier was excited because tonight was the night he hoped the evil magic would be undone and his nephew would return to life. While the party guests talked and joked and laughed together, Dr Drosselmeier set about emptying the huge bag he had brought with him. It was filled with gingerbread and shortcake, candy walking sticks and sugar pigs, nuts and bon bons, nougat and humbugs . . . High and low, in every corner of the room, Dr Drosselmeier heaped piles of all the Mouse King's favourite things to eat. *That should tempt him out from wherever he's hiding*, thought Dr Drosselmeier, determinedly.

Then it was time to give Clara her Christmas present. The little girl's eyes opened wide with excitement as she stripped off the sparkly paper. But her face suddenly fell as she saw the ugly nutcracker prince. Then, gently, Clara stroked the doll's face. He wasn't cute, he wasn't cuddly – he wasn't even new! But that was exactly why Clara decided she loved him. She couldn't bear to think of leaving him all alone, laughed at and unloved – especially at Christmas time. Clara clutched the nutcracker prince close to her and hugged him tight. And Dr Drosselmeier slipped away from the party, his heart light with hope . . .

When the party was over and it was bedtime at last, Clara tucked the wooden doll up next to her. "I love you," she whispered, just before she fell asleep. "I'll look after you always." And that night, Clara had a very strange dream. She dreamt that the nutcracker prince woke up beside her. He smiled at Clara and held her hand, and led her downstairs. There was scuffling and squeaking coming from the drawing room, and when Clara peeped around the door she saw a terrible sight. There were mice everywhere! They were climbing all over Dr Drosselmeier's goodies, fighting and biting each other to get at the sweets. And worst of all, a horrible seven-headed mouse was standing in the middle of the carpet, cackling with glee at all the arguing and the mess. The seven-headed mouse wore seven golden crowns and Clara could tell at once that he must be the king of the evil creatures.

Very bravely, the nutcracker prince charged at the gruesome Mouse King with a sword glinting in his hand and began to fight furiously. But he was completely outnumbered. The mice swarmed to their king's defence. They dragged the nutcracker prince to the ground and he disappeared under a thousand biting, clawing bodies. Just as the Mouse King threw back his head and began to laugh, Clara tore her slipper off her foot and threw it at him with all her might. WHAM! It hit the Mouse King on four of his seven horrible heads. He staggered to and fro for a second, and then collapsed dead to the floor.

As soon as the mice saw that their leader was no more, their courage deserted them. They hurried to scoop up his body and then they were gone, streaming off through cracks in the wall, holes in the skirting and gaps in the floorboards.

The nutcracker prince ran to Clara and kissed her. "Thank you for all you have done for me," he whispered, and there were tears sparkling in his painted eyes. "Let me repay you by taking you on a wonderful journey to my kingdom, the realm of sweets . . ."

It was the most wonderful dream Clara had ever had. She travelled through forests made of barley sugar, crossed rivers that ran with lemonade, picked flowers of sherbert, walked on paths of chocolate, and visited the nutcracker prince's gingerbread castle. In fact, Clara was very sorry to be woken up – even though it was Christmas Day itself! She hugged the wooden doll and told him, "You're the best present I've ever had," and she could have sworn that his smile was even broader than usual.

Meanwhile, across the city, Dr Drosselmeier had also woken up to find the best present he'd ever had. There sprawled underneath his Christmas tree, sleeping an exhausted but peaceful sleep, was his brave, handsome nephew . . .

THE FISHERMAN AND THE BOTTLE

a tale from The Arabian Nights

The fisherman was having a very bad day. The first time he had cast his nets in to the Arabian Sea, all he had pulled out was an old boot. The second time, all he had pulled out was a broken pot full of mud. The third time he had cast his nets, and all he had pulled in was an old copper bottle. But there was something about the bottle that stopped the fisherman from hurling it back into the deeps. Perhaps it was the way the stopper glinted in the light. Or maybe it was the strange wax seal around the neck, highly decorated with strange markings. It might even have been the fact that the fisherman could have sworn he heard a faint noise coming from inside. In any case, something made the fisherman plunge his hand into his pocket for his penknife, slash the wax seal around the neck, and draw out the heavy stopper.

The fisherman turned the copper bottle upside down and shook it. All that came out was a trickle of dust as fine as sand . . . a trickle of dust that seemed to blow upwards with the wind, instead of falling down . . . a trickle of dust that became a wisp of smoke . . . a wisp of smoke that became a puff of mist . . . a puff of mist that

became a cloud
billowing overhead . . . a cloud
that formed huge feet and legs, and an
enormous body, and strong arms and hands –
and a massive, fierce, bald head with golden earrings
and a long moustache and cruel eyes. In other words, there
was a gigantic genie towering over him.

"Kneel before me, you spawn of a quivering jellyfish!" the
genie roared. "And prepare to meet your death!"

"What have I done?" the terrified fisherman begged, falling to
the sand. "I know the story of Aladdin and the genie of the lamp.
Haven't I set you free? Aren't you meant to grant me wishes?"

"You have indeed set me free," the gigantic genie bellowed,
"but it is FAR TOO LATE for wishes! For the first hundred years that
I was trapped inside that copper prison, I did indeed swear that I
would grant three wishes to anyone who set me free – no matter
how greedy they were. But no one helped me, and I grew
impatient. For the next two hundred years, I swore that I would
give never-ending riches to anyone who set me free. But no one
helped me, and I grew angry. For the next five hundred years, I

swore that I would give an entire kingdom to anyone who set me free. But no one helped me – and I grew furious. It was then that I swore that the very next person I saw would taste my revenge. Now I have been trapped inside that copper prison for TWO THOUSAND YEARS. And it is you who will have the honour of receiving my punishment!"

The fisherman shuddered as the genie drew an enormous, shining, curved sword from his belt. He began to think fast if there were some way he could save himself . . .

To the genie's astonishment, the fisherman gave a friendly wink. "Come on now," the fisherman smirked, "enough of this fooling around. The way you appeared from nowhere like that was really very impressive, but I should tell you that I simply don't believe in magic."

"What do you mean, you don't believe in magic?" the genie roared, his face as black as soot.

"Well, sorcerers and genies and spells – no one believes in all that old rubbish nowadays," sniggered the fisherman, scornfully.

"Old rubbish!" blustered the genie, quite lost for words.

"So we've both had a bit of a laugh and a joke, haven't we?" continued the fisherman, quite calmly. "Now, you just tell me where you hid to make it look like you came out of the bottle, and I'll congratulate you on your fantastic trick. Then you can tell me where you're going to perform your conjuring show next time and I'll promise to bring lots of gullible friends who'll pay good money to watch you. And then we'll both shake hands on it and go home to our wives. What do you say?"

"How dare you call me a fake!" boomed the raging genie, as green smoke hissed out of his ears. "I'll show you that I'm real! I'll show you that I'm the most terrifying genie that ever came out of a bottle – I'll prove it to you, by getting back into it right now!"

Suddenly the genie's massive face began to melt, his arms and legs began to blur, his huge body began to shimmer in the air. His features became formless and shifting like a great cloud of mist. Then the cloud narrowed into a spiral of smoke that funnelled round and down and round and down . . . and right into the neck of the bottle. As the very last wisp disappeared inside, the fisherman grabbed the heavy stopper and rammed it into the neck of the bottle as hard as he could.

"I shall never cast another net as long as I live," gasped the sweating fisherman, and he hurled the bottle as far as he could out into the ocean.

So if you're ever at the beach and you see a copper bottle bobbing about in the water or washed up on the shore, be very careful before you open it, won't you . . .